Payton is A of Dirt

BY SHANNA SIMPSON

ILLUSTRATED BY
IDMARY HERNANDEZ

Payton is Afraid of Dirt

All marketing and publishing rights guaranteed to and reserved by:

721 W. Abram St. Arlington, TX 76013
Toll-free: 800·489·0727 | Fax: 817·277·2270
www.FHautism.com | info@FHautism.com

Text © 2017 Shanna Simpson
Illustrations © 2017 Idmary Hernandez
All rights reserved.
Printed in Canada.

No part of this product may be reproduced in any manner whatsoever without written permission of Future Horizons, except in the case of brief quotations embodied in reviews.

ISBN: 9781941765579

Payton was scared of being dirty.

He washed in the kitchen for a long time.

He washed in the bathtub for a long time.

He rubbed ... and he scrubbed.

Payton cleaned his toys all the time.

And he straightened his room even when it was spic and span.

Payton's family worried.

Dad said, "Why are you cleaning your room so much?"

Mom and Emily said, "Payton, what's wrong?"

"I can't stop cleaning," Payton replied.

"I can't stop thinking about how dirty everything is. What's happening to me?"

Payton tried playing catch with his friend Jake.

But every time Jake threw the ball,
Payton thought, This ball has too much dirt on it!
If I touch it, I will get really sick!

Payton tried ignoring the thought.

That didn't work.
The ball always flew through the air and plunked at his feet.

Jake stitched his eyebrows together in confusion.

"We've played this since kindergarten. Why aren't you doing anything?"

"I don't know," Payton whispered.

"You're such a baby," Jake yelled.

"I'm going home!" He picked up the baseball and stomped off.

Payton ran home.

"I don't know how to stop doing it!" he yelled.

He rushed into his mother's arms.

"It's okay, buddy," said Dad. "We'll figure this out."

Payton hoped so.

At breakfast, Dad told Payton they were taking him to a psychiatrist, a special doctor for the brain.

Payton nodded, trying not to look scared.

Mom took Payton to see the doctor.

Payton tried reading his favorite book while they waited, but the thoughts kept swirling around in his head.

"What's wrong with me, Mom?"

His mother put an arm around him.

"We don't know yet."

Mom and Payton followed the nurse into the office.

Bright colors filled the walls. Payton saw crayons on a table.

He felt a lot better, so he wiped off a chair and sat down at the table just as a tall man entered the room.

"I'm Doctor LaBock," he said. "Mind if I sit across from you, Payton?" asked Doctor LaBock.

"Okay," said Payton.

The doctor smiled back at him and sat down.

"I heard there's somebody in your head bossing you around."

Payton nodded. His feet swung back and forth under the big chair.

He felt like a thousand baby birds were fluttering in his stomach.

It tells me if I touch something dirty I might get sick, or I might get somebody else sick."

The doctor nodded.

Yes," said Payton. "Sometimes it says, 'You will get a disease if you don't clean your room right now!' If I don't do that, it says to go wash my hands right away.

I have to do what it says even though it doesn't make sense."

Doctor LaBock thanked Payton and sent him into the waiting room while Mom talked to the doctor alone.

Payton tried reading again. His hands shook until the nurse called him back into the doctor's office.

Doctor LaBock said, "Payton, I think you might have OCD. Do you know what that means?"

Payton shook his head.

"Well," said the doctor, "OCD stands for Obsessive-Compulsive Disorder. It's something a lot of people have. OCD makes them worry and worry about all different things."

"In order to get rid of their fears, they sometimes wash their hands. Only, they spend so much time cleaning, they don't have time to do other things."

"Like play with toys?" Payton asked.

He understood a little better now.

"Yes, like play with toys."

"Will I make other people get sick?" Payton asked.

He didn't want anyone else to catch OCD.

"No, it is not contagious," said the doctor. "That means you can't give it to anyone else. It's not like a cold or the chicken pox."

"My friend Jake doesn't understand why I can't play catch with him anymore. Will I ever pick up a baseball again if I always have OCD?" Payton asked his mother.

"It might take a little practice, but we'll work together to help you not be so afraid of getting sick," said Doctor LaBock.

Payton nodded. "Okay." There was still a lump in his throat.

"Does it get better?" Mom asked.

"There are things you can learn to help you feel better," said the doctor.

"Sometimes people take medicine, but not always. We will have to find the best way."

He handed Payton's mom a paper. Mom showed Payton the paper.

"There are other kids who have OCD just like you. They wrote down some tricks that help them feel better."

"I put my worries in a special box," wrote Kaylee.

"I like to take walks with my dog. Then I forget my nervous thoughts. Your friend, Sarah."

A boy named Tyler said, "I used to wash my hands a lot, but now I write funny stories about my OCD instead. When I laugh at my thoughts, they get smaller."

At last, Mom read, "You are not alone."

She hugged Payton for a long, long time.

"I challenge you, Payton," said the doctor, "to come up with something of your own that makes your OCD get a little bit smaller. You may still have some thoughts, but you might not have as many as you do now."

He handed Payton a workbook.

"I want you to read this with your parents, okay?"

Payton nodded.

They said "goodbye" and "see you next week."

That night, the whole family read Doctor LaBock's workbook.

The book helped Payton learn new ways to fight OCD.

Payton thought hard about what Dr. LaBock said.

How could he make OCD smaller?

Well, he could put his OCD in a shrinking machine.

When his thought said, "You'll get a cold if you don't clean your room," Payton imagined the machine making an OCD monster get smaller and smaller until it was a teeny speck.

He still cleaned his room ... but only a little.

Sometimes, he made up a funny story about OCD.

Payton grew stronger and stronger!

"You're not washing as much," said Dad one afternoon.

Payton grinned. "Tomorrow I'm picking up a baseball."

"Alright," said Dad, smiling.

The next morning, OCD yelled in Payton's ears. "All this dirt will make you sick!"

Then, he cleaned his room, his toys, and his hands until …

"Boo!" said Emily, from inside Payton's closet.

Payton jumped.

He made the scariest face he could.

Emily ran out of the room!

Then, he had an idea.

The next time OCD came around, he'd ROAR it away!

Payton scared or shrunk OCD whenever it bugged him.

He fought OCD every way he could.

After a while, he got good at it.

He didn't wash his toys every day. His room stayed messy … most of the time.

Mom reminded him every day, "You are not alone. We love you, Payton."

Payton played catch with Jake. And sometimes, just sometimes, they decided it was okay to get really, really dirty!

ABOUT THE AUTHOR

Shanna was born and raised in Chicago's southwestern suburbs where she earned her degree in journalism from North Central College in Naperville, IL.

At age seven, Shanna was diagnosed with Obsessive Compulsive Disorder (OCD), which motivated her to share her experiences in a picture book about coping with OCD as a child.

Besides her day job at the library and several other writing projects, Shanna enjoys time with her family and dogs, Kallie and Jordan, and has been a serious Chicago Cubs fan since attending her first game in 1989 at age three.